ASH MONKEY GOES TO THE DOCTOR

AUTHOR: JILLIA WEINBERGER

Dedicated by Jason and Asher Weinberger in loving memory of Jillia and her dream

ASH MONKEY GOES TO THE DOCTOR

TO MY SWEET ASHER AND ALL KIDDOS EVERYWHERE

WHO NEED AN EXTRA HUG WHEN THEY GO

TO THE DOCTOR.

ASH MONKEY GOES TO THE DOCTOR

THIS BOOK BELONGS TO

ASH MONKEY GOES TO THE DOCTOR

NO PART OF THIS BOOK MAY BE REPRODUCED

IN ANY FORM WITHOUT WRITTEN

PERMISSION FROM THE PUBLISHER, EXCEPT FOR

BRIEF PASSAGES INCLUDED IN A REVIEW.

Early one morning, Ash

Monkey woke up feeling yucky.

"Mommy," Ash said. "I don't feel so good."

"What's wrong?" asked Mommy.

"My ears are hot and itchy," said Ash.

"Sounds like we need to take a trip to

see Doctor See," said Mommy.

"But I don't want to go to the doctor! I'm scared!"protested Ash. "It's OK, Ash," said Mommy. "I can tell you exactly what Doctor See will do, so it doesn't seem so scary."

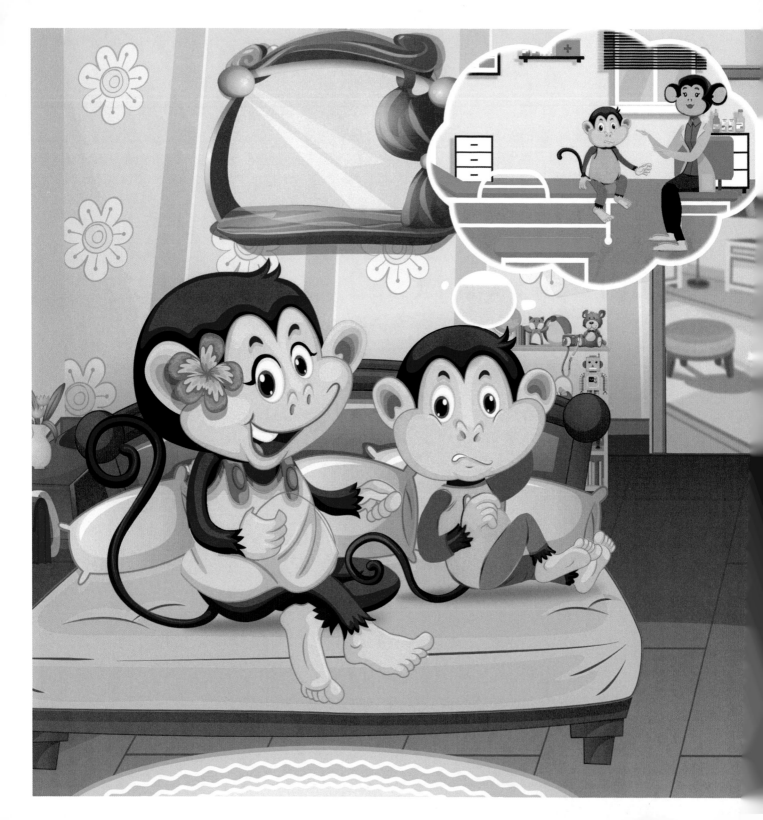

"Doctor See is going to take your temperature, listen to your chest, look inside your mouth, and look inside your ears.

And that's it!" said Mommy.

"But I am scared it will hurt," said Ash.

"Would Mommy let someone hurt you?"

asked Mommy. "No," said Ash. "That's right.

Doctor See is our friend and is going

to make you feel all better!" said Mommy.

Mommy and Ash got in their banana car and drove through the forest to see the doctor. When they got there, Doctor See was waiting for them with a big smile.

Doctor See did exactly what Mommy said she would. She took Ash's temperature, looked inside his mouth, listened to his chest, and looked inside his ears. "Looks like you have an ear infection," said Doctor See. "But don't worry, I will give you some medicine and it will make you feel all better!"

When the visit was over, Mommy and Ash Monkey went back to their treehouse. "Mommy, you were right. That wasn't bad at all," said Ash. "I told you, sweetie. Mommy would never let anything bad happen to you," said Mommy.

"I love you, Mommy," said Ash.

"I love you, too," said Mommy.

ASH MONKEY GOES TO THE DOCTOR

CONTACT US

EMAIL: JILLIA.WEINB@GMAIL.COM
INSTAGRAM: MOMMYLIFEFUN

Made in the USA
Middletown, DE
20 October 2022